Usborne Fairytale Sticker Stories

Rumpelstiltskin

Illustrated by Stephen Cartwright

Retold by Heather Amery and Sarah Khan

How to use this book

This book tells the story of Rumpelstiltskin.
Some words in the story have been replaced by pictures.
Find the stickers that match these pictures and stick them over the top.
Each sticker has the word with it to help you read the story.

Some of the big pictures have pieces missing.
Find the stickers with the missing pieces to finish the pictures.

A yellow duck is hidden in every picture. When you have found
the duck you can put a ⬤ sticker on the page.

Once, a miller had a clever daughter.

The  boasted about her to the King.

"My daughter is so clever she can even spin straw into gold." The  wanted to see.

2

The daughter went to the King's palace.

The King took her to a room with a  , a

spinning wheel, and some  . "Spin it

into gold by morning, or you will die," he said.

The daughter sat down and cried.

She couldn't spin  into gold. Then a

little man came in. "What will you give me if I

spin your straw into  ?" he asked.

"I'll give you my necklace," she said.

The little man sat at the  . By

morning, he had spun all the straw into gold

thread. He took the 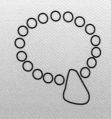 and disappeared.

5

The King was very pleased.

He took the 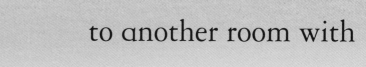 to another room with

a bigger pile of straw. "Spin this

into gold by morning, or you'll die," he said.

6

The little man appeared again.

"What will you give me if I spin this bigger pile

of straw into 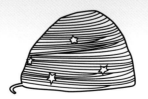 ?" he asked. "I'll

give you my ring," said the  .

In the morning the King came back.

The little man had taken the and spun

the straw into gold. The King was pleased. But

he was greedy and wanted more  .

miller

I found the duck!

stool

straw

I found the duck!

I found the duck!

messenger

little man

I found the duck!

gold

baby

little man

daughter

Queen

I found the duck!

gold

Queen

straw

daughter

little man

Queen

baby

gold

King

I found the duck!

I found the duck!

I found the duck!

I found the duck!

I found the duck!

Queen

little man

straw

daughter

gold

I found the duck!

I found the duck!

straw

King

I found the duck!

ring

necklace

spinning wheel

foot

He took the daughter to a bigger room.

An even bigger pile of  was inside.

"Spin it into gold by morning, or you'll die," said

the  . The little man came again.

"What will you give me now?" he asked.

"I've nothing left," said the  .

"Promise to give me your first baby when

you're Queen," said the .

10

In the morning, the King was delighted.

"Marry me, and we'll always have lots of

," he said. Soon there was a royal

wedding and the daughter was  .

A year later, the Queen had a baby.

She was very happy. But then, the

came. "If you can't guess my name in three days,

I'll take your  away," he said.

The Queen thought all day and night.

When the little man came the next day, the

 asked, "Is your name John or Henry?"

"No, you're wrong," said the  .

13

The little man came again the next day.

"Is it Bandylegs, Crooksy or Boggles?" asked

the  . "No. One more try and I'll

take away the  ," said the little man.

The next day, a messenger came.

"I saw a little man in the woods," said the

 , "He was singing, 'My name is

Rumpelstiltskin.'" The  was pleased.

15

"You're Rumpelstiltskin," said the Queen.

The  was angry. He stamped his

 very hard and disappeared forever.

Cover design by Michael Hill   Digital manipulation by Keith Furnival

First published in 2006 by Usborne Publishing Ltd, Usborne House, 83-85 Saffron Hill, London EC1N 8RT, England. www.usborne.com